Fire of passion

10 erotic short stories

VALLEETSY

SCAN ME

*This book is only for those
who have the courage
to explore the boundaries
of eroticism and discover
their hidden
desires.*

The important things first

Immerse yourself in a sensual world of seductive passion brought to life in this enchanting masterpiece.
This book will captivate you with its captivating story that magically combines fervent lust, burning desire and devoted devotion.
The words in this work have been carefully chosen to awaken your senses and stimulate your imagination.
With provocative descriptions, it takes you into the depths of human lust and lets you feel the tingling eroticism on every page.
Only for those who have the courage to explore the boundaries of eroticism and discover their hidden desires, this book is made.
It is a work that will speak to your most intimate dreams and ignite your deepest desires as you plunge into the dangerously tormenting maelstrom of passion..

Table of contents

FIRE OF PASSION 1

10 EROTIC SHORT STORIES 1

MASTER FLIGHT 13

AWESOME RIDE HOME 39

ANOTHER LESSON 52

THE SEARCH FOR THE LIMITS 57

THE OLD MAN 75

THE KEGEL EVENING 87

MY FIRST ASS FUCK 92

AWESOME HOTEL STAY 98

HOTELBOY..121

about the author 132

MASTER FLIGHT

Her master's order came via email.
'Tie off your tits, take the hose clamps, but carefully, clamp your cunt with the wide metal clamps and push a cock in first. You know which ones I like. Business dress. Ban on speaking! Bring handcuffs and the small steel rod. In four hours you'll be on my mat. And put this email in your pocket!'
500 km in four hours. Ina had to fly. She was prepared for these last-minute appointments. Everything was ready in her playroom. She screwed the hose clamps tight so that she could just about stand it and also please her master.

The special screwdriver for this disappeared into her handbag.
She chose the ribbed steel dildo, extra thick, and placed the ordered clamp in her cunt

flaps. She could already feel a slight burning sensation in her udders. ,Well, that'll be fun'. White blouse, knee-length skirt, jacket, heels and thong, that's how her lord and master liked her. On the back of the printed email she wrote quickly To the airport please! and One ticket to Hamburg, please, one way. She wasn't allowed to speak!
Ina didn't forget the sturdy stainless steel handcuffs or this little snappy rod with the very thin wires.
She ran to the nearest taxi rank, showed the driver her note and rather carelessly jumped into the back seat. She had completely forgotten about the clamps on her cunt and had to regret it sorely. During the 20-minute drive she calmed down a bit. She was concentrating on her aching cunt when her vision almost went black. The security check.

'That pig, blackmailer, I'll bite your tail off and chew your balls.' But it's of no use to her. If she doesn't fly now, the revenge would be terrible. She knew her master, his impatience, his short temper. Security check on all that metal. She had to go through it whether she wanted to or not.

She nervously bought the ticket and had to hurry. The flight would be called soon. There was no way she could miss her flight. She rushed to security. There wasn't much going on this morning. She was completely insecure.
What would happen right now. It was unlikely that she would be waved through.
Everything looked like routine at first. Bag on the band, the jacket with it. Then through the security gate and of course it started immediately. The LEDs on the body scanner told the security woman where metallic objects were likely to be found.
"May I?" She began to feel Ina without hesitation. First the shoulders, the upper arms, forearms. She was then asked to stretch her arms to the sides.

Back, flanks, hips, legs. She got the ring-shaped hand scanner and started scanning the more intimate parts, which of course made a loud impact on her tits.
"What is that, what do you have there?"
Ina remained silent, hooked her teeth into the side of her lower lip and looked down embarrassed.

"What do you have there?" the security officer repeated. This time a little more impatient and louder.

Ina was silent.

"May I ask you to come with me! You can take the bag and your jacket with you."

Ina took her utensils from the conveyor belt and walked ahead of the officer.

"The question again, what have you hidden there?"

Ina remained silent. "Take off the blouse!" This tone seemed like a command and Ina had learned to react to commands immediately. Quickly but unhurriedly, she unbuttoned her blouse and presented her severed udders to the woman's astonished face.

She whistled softly through her teeth. "Gerd, come here!" She's actually not allowed to do that; men are not allowed to strip search women. "Have you seen anything like this?"

The security officer who had been summoned entered the barren room. He stared transfixed at her tits. Of course he had seen something like this before, on the Internet.

"No, nothing like that," he lied, "doesn't that hurt?" He looked into Ina's face. This made Ina uncomfortable, but what could she do about it. She was only carrying out her master's orders. She shook her head. She lied too. His hand approached the different sized tits and grabbed the larger one.
"Gerd, you're not allowed to do that, it's against the rules!"
"Leave me alone with your rules. You shouldn't have called me either. There was no danger for you. Call Harry in and close the door from the outside," the colleague was dispatched.
Completely perplexed, she left the room, which the next moment another man in uniform entered. "What kind of pigeon do we have here?" he greeted Ina. "Here, have you seen that before?" "Constricted tits, I don't believe it!" He now reached into the udder flesh, the smaller one, and squeezed just as hard. Ina didn't move, she was used to worse.
"First look in the bag, I saw something on the screen." He took the bag and turned it over. The entire contents tumbled onto the table. Handcuffs, credit card, change, ticket,

screwdriver, keys, boarding pass, whip and the email from her master.

"That's interesting, read the email." Ina's face turned red.

"Read out loud!"

"Tie off your tits, take the hose clamps, but carefully, clamp your cunt with the wide metal clamps and push a cock in you first. You know which ones I like. Business dress. Ban on speaking! Bring handcuffs and the small steel rod. In four hours you'll be on my mat. And put this email in your pocket! Hey, that's a slave and what a slave she is."

"Take off your clothes now!" Harry narrowed his eyes and pressed the command between his lips. "Is it going to happen soon or do you need tutoring?" Harry reached for the steel rod. That worked. In a flash, all the clothes were on the floor and Ina folded her arms behind her head and spread her legs wide, just as she always does when standing in front of her master, still in the open front door.

"We should stick to the rules!" Harry winked at Gerd.

"And they say…?"

"Everything needs to be examined!" Harry laughed.

"Gerd get the long, thin needles out of the cupboard, the ones we recently took from a surgeon."
Harry first stabbed her big udder. At first very slowly and only superficially, as if he was expecting some liquid substance to be about to squirt out. Again and again he pulled the needle all the way out so that he could push it in even deeper the next time. Harry's hand became like a hammer. Ina kept her eyes closed and moaned loudly all the time. Small drops of blood formed in several places on the udder skin. If the needle had been a knife, Ina's tits would have been completely shredded.

"I don't think there's anything in it. But lift up the flesh by the nipples, maybe there's something on the underside." Gerd didn't need to be told twice and Harry continued his work from below. With every stitch the needle came out at the top.

"She has such big warts that if you poke her tits, you usually always hit the wart. "It's rare to see a warthog like that," said Gerd happily, who now hoped to get his hands on it. According to the hierarchy, he was entitled to the small udder.

"Gerd should get the knitting needles from dear grandma the other day, who cried so much when she had to leave her needles behind."
Gerd stood in front of Ina with two knitting needles. They were thick needles. You could knit a winter sweater with them and so that the long needles wouldn't dance around and hurt anyone, they were flexible in the end. There was a small lump at the very end. This prevented the stitches from falling down.
"The little udder is yours, so let's go! Start now, otherwise the bitch will miss her flight!"
Ina didn't like hearing that about the missed flight. She was still standing there in her slave position. Both of them only had their tits in mind. How much she would have liked to feel relief in her cunt, which she almost didn't feel anymore.
Gerd's eyes sparkled. Finally he was allowed. The sadist in him literally blossomed. He took both needles in his hand and rubbed Ina's tit with the flexible parts. Clear traces could be seen.
"May I give you some support, Gerd?"
Without waiting for an answer, he took the steel rod in his hand and hit her naked ass with full force.

Ina's ass was more sensitive than her udders and she screamed. She did not expect that. Four or five times the whip landed on the intended target called the ass. In no time it was bloodshot.

"Thanks, but now full concentration. This also applies to you, you pig! Just stand there."

Gerd took the nipple of her little tit hard in his fingers, lifted it and drove the needle through the udder meat from below so that it came out again at the top.

Ina was in pain, tremendous pain, even though she gets her tits trained again and again and also trains herself. The pain of the puncture was still bearable, even though the skin offered resistance. But the slow progress in the flesh and, above all, the resistance when exiting, bothered her more than she would have liked. But she endured it for her master, albeit loudly.

Gerd still had the other knitting needle. He drove it just as slowly and seemingly carefully, but this time from above into the fatty tissue until it emerged again at the bottom. This time he pulled the needle further through to the end of the flexible extension.

"I would have liked to have done that with the big udder too! That looks so cool."

"You can still do it! Wait! Hold her teat!" Gerd pulled the needle that he had just driven in a little bit back to the actual needle. "Breathe in!" he ordered Ina. He took the knitting needle in both hands and looked Ina in the face. Ina turned pale, she knew what was about to come. Gerd looked for a secure footing. "Hold on tight, Harry!" His gaze didn't let go of Ina. He lifted both hands a little and with a powerful pull, the nub at the end of the embroidery device was pulled through the udder fat, so quickly that it took quite a while for it to bleed.

Ina opened her eyes. The whites of her eyes stood out clearly and looked almost like Louis Armstrong's when he played his trumpet solo. At the same time, she opened her mouth so that one had to be afraid that the corners of her mouth would tear. She wanted to scream, to scream forcefully, the pain was so bad. But she couldn't. The scream caught in her throat. For a few seconds it was quiet, dead quiet. But then it burst out of her with force. The scream was so loud that Harry had to cover her mouth. Ina screamed and screamed. She barely breathed in between. Her breath caught in her throat again and again. She forced out air even though her mouth was wide open. The screams became more long-lasting. She had found her breathing rate again. Now guttural sounds came from her mouth. It sounded like screaming and moaning at the same moment. She reflexively closed her mouth to swallow her saliva and lost her breathing rhythm again.

Gerd, this sadist grinned thievingly. He has now given it to the bitch. She's had enough for quite a while.

"Harry, I think her udders are clean. We should let them on board. "

„Soooo!?"

"Of course not!" Gerd had now gained the upper hand and Harry acknowledged this without envy. Harry got a bottle of iodine to disinfect the bleeding wound and also very politely pulled out the other knitting needle. They left the big tit alone. This slave bitch had really had enough. She could barely stand on her feet. The iodine was a balm for her wound, which burned terribly, but it was nothing compared to the pain from before.

"Get dressed!" Ina took her thong first and was about to get into it. "I thought slaves weren't allowed to wear underwear? Stick it in your ass!", which Ina immediately obediently did. "You can leave the 'bra' on, but not so sloppily, you pig." Gerd took the screwdriver and tightened it a little more. Now he was satisfied.

"And the 'panties' don't fit properly either." He adjusted the clamp on her cunt until he thought it fit well.

Ina got fully dressed, packed her bag and wanted to leave the room.

"Not like that, my love! We haven't examined your shoes yet. But then your plane left." Ina took off her shoes and then had to go barefoot. "And who gave you permission to put on the blouse? Not us!" These were again those typical slave games that she loved on the one hand, but also totally hated. ,That's unfair!' But she remained silent and left her blouse as a souvenir for the security guards.

"Hands behind your back!" She heard the clacking of the handcuffs and one of the two put the handle of the handbag in her mouth. "It's pretty warm today. Come on, I'll open your jacket for you! Harry, tell the airline, someone else is coming for flight 326."

As she was being taken to the plane, Ina heard Harry speaking into the cell phone: "She's sitting in the first row, colleague."

It continues, with a decent amount of torment, sarcasm and gallows humor.
Have fun and of course "Don't repeat it!" or do you?
Colleague? Ina was sure that her colleague was her master. She knew little about him privately, only that he was involved in aviation. It would be a very bumpy flight, she was sure.
Ina was the last to board the plane and was already greeted by the stewardess.
"So you're our VIP," and looked at her disparagingly from top to bottom and back again. Ina lowered her gaze, as she had learned, and just nodded, embarrassed and barely visible.
"Immediately to the left, middle seat and buckle up, we're about to start," came from her thin lips in a commanding tone. Ina only thought about the other passengers who were about to stare at her, but to her surprise the business class was empty. Not a soul. Holiday season!! The economy passengers sat behind the dividing curtain. Ina breathed a sigh of relief. But at the same moment she jumped again. She thought of the stewardess' imperious look and the familiar you.

"Fasten your seat belt!"
What if her hands were in handcuffs and she surreptitiously showed her flashing cuffs to the flight attendant.
“Ladies and gentlemen, your captain. We have not yet received permission from the tower to start the engines. We expect it in about 15 minutes. In the meantime, make yourself comfortable on board. You can use your cell phones again until you leave our parking position.”
„Ladies and Gentlemen …“
“So my little pigeon, then we'll strap you in. We have a few minutes and you can rest assured that you will fly safely, like in Abraham's lap. We will make sure of that now.”
"Peter! Would you please come to the front of the room with me,” she called to her colleague on the on-board telephone.
“Can you help me tie her up properly, erm, I mean buckle her up, of course,” she greeted her colleague with a grin.
“But yes, dearest colleague,” Peter grinned back, “what are you planning to do?”
Ina believed that there were only sadists left in the world. The two of them had free rein

and she was sure she wouldn't be able to move an inch during the flight.

"What do you think if we undress you now and you experience your first naked flight? Get up, put your skirt down!" Jutta, the flight attendant didn't hesitate and the blue skirt was already lying on the cabin floor. Peter pushed the blazer off her shoulders until it caught on her handcuffs.

Both flight attendants whistled appreciatively through their teeth when they saw Ina's already reddened, large tits with the puncture marks and even discovered the small, inconspicuous rings in her nipples. "I think she can handle something. Bend over, you stoop!" Peter stepped into the second row, took Ina by the jacket and threaded her arms around the back of her airplane seat. As is well known, the spaces between the individual seats are quite narrow and the two of them had to use a bit of force to squeeze them in. With rough force, Ina was pushed into the seat by her shoulders. From the front it really looked like she was stark naked.

"Legs up and feet on the seat!"

Ina couldn't do it on her own. Her upper body was bent too far forward because the two flying sadists had folded up the armrests between the seats.

"Do you have to do everything yourself?" The stewardess brought a foot onto the seat and stuck it into the narrow crack between the seat and the back of the next seat. Peter did the same with the other foot. Both feet were then pulled outwards, thereby opening her thighs wide. The crack was so narrow that there was no escape from her tense position. "What do we have here?" asked Peter when he saw Ina's cunt. He grabbed the clip and Ina let out a suppressed howl. The pressure was already hurting her, now the pulling pain was added to it. "Tear them off!" demanded Jutta, who was now standing in the second row behind Ina. Peter pulled the steel clamp very carefully with slight twists and painfully slowly for Ina. Her lobes were stretched to the limit and she had no illusions that Peter would open the clamp.

Then everything went very fast. The clamp tore off the cunt flaps and Ina was about to open her mouth to scream loudly when Jutta forcefully closed her mouth from behind. Her eyes were almost as big as they had been with the knitting needle. The next moment the steel dildo slipped, no, one had to say, shot out of her soaking wet cunt and fell at Peter's feet. It's no secret that slaves are always wet, and have to be wet. But Ina was wet, always wet and then there were her strong inner cunt muscles, which in this case had the effect of a catapult.

"Can't you warn me, you pig, you cunt bomber?" Peter smacked her right and left in the face, really hard. Jutta, who was already standing behind Ina, grabbed both ears and held Ina as if in a vice. "Keep going, Peter, you're in such a good mood right now and you cunt bomb aren't making a peep anymore! Understood?"

Jutta made nodding movements with Ina's head. And then Peter started. First right, then left. First five in rhythm and then single blows, eight at once on the left, then right again. Ina didn't count and if she did, then only on command. But there must have been 50 to 60. Ina's cheeks burned and her whole face hurt. Her brain appeared to have suffered no impairment, thanks to Jutta.

"What do we do with this pussy bomb now?

"Put it back?" asked Peter and casually pinched the cunt clamp into Ina's big udder.

"It's best to put them in the autoclave (steamer). Then it's nice and hot when we start and we save ourselves having to heat the business." Peter was already in the galley (galley) when Jutta called after him. "Bring wipes!"

When Peter brought the cloths, he saw Jutta kneeling on the floor. Both hands were in Ina's big cunt and moved as if she was washing her hands in them.

"Here to dry off!"

"But not for me, my darling." Jutta stood up and ran her hands through Peter's black hair. "So that your wife also gets something from her and maybe one or two passengers in the wooden class will want to eat you if you smell like pussy. No, I need the towels for her cunt. It should be nice and dry when we push the hot bomb back into its barrel.

Now it was Peter who, without saying a word, knelt down, stuffed the tea towel into Ina's cunt and turned it as if he were cleaning a cognac glass. Completely soaked, he pulled it out and held it in front of Jutta's nose.

"Are you that wet yet?"

"Nesser!"

Jutta reached under her skirt, took off her panties and ran them through the crack again. "I think we would have to stuff this Pottsau's mouth with it so that she doesn't

scream too much when her cunt gets visitors."
"Open your mouth and woe betide you if you spit it out!"
Ina immediately and without hesitation opened her slave mouth and was now allowed to enjoy the pussy juice from a Stewar nozzle.
"Ladies and gentlemen, your captain. We have just received permission to start the engines. It's starting right now. Please turn off your cell phones again and fasten your seatbelts. I'll get back to you shortly after takeoff with some information about our flight. Thank you very much."
„Ladies and Gentlemen …"
"And you just sit here as quiet as a mouse."
'Idiot!', Ina thought to herself.
After the well-known gymnastics exercises for the safety of the passengers, which no one paid any attention to anyway, unless the stewardess is pretty, Jutta took her seat opposite Ina. The plane taxied to the runway. The curtain between business and eco cannot remain closed during takeoff and landing. But Jutta sat in her prescribed position, which was visible from the business class but not from the eco.

So she took the opportunity and pulled up her skirt, spread her legs and jerked off. Jutta's eyes were focused on Ina. She literally pierced her with her gaze. What fascinated her most were the tied udders of different sizes with the huge warts on them, which were also different sizes. And she was also impressed by the many birthmarks. 'Those at the Inquisition would have had a lot to do with that.' thought Jutta. While she was jerking off, she also remembered the numbers game, where dots have to be connected with lines to form a picture. But with this sow she would use a needle or a small knife.

Her eyes fell on Ina's stomach. Because of the uncomfortable position, her stomach was not taut as usual, but showed a slight fold of skin. They will change that as soon as they are in the air.

"Shit, that cunt!" Ina only saw the movement of her mouth because the engines were roaring and the plane was getting faster and faster. Jutta forgot the steel dildo in the autoclave. 'Well wait, as soon as we get to the top, put it in the cunt cannon.' Maybe that was better, because the scream was definitely heard on the ground. Now the engines were loud.

Jutta was jerking off and really wanted to reach orgasm before the seatbelt signs went out. She was already using her second hand. The fingers rubbed her cunt nipple hard and three fingers of the other hand were in her hole. She climaxed just as the seatbelt sign went out. It's a shitty feeling when you can't fully enjoy the orgasm. But she had to get up immediately and prepare for service for the short flight. And her colleague was already on the way. Peter knew what a rotten pig she was, but still, he didn't have to know everything.

"Put that thing in her, quickly, I forgot. And we have a full house in the back, come on, hurry up. Take your gloves, this thing is hot."

Peter came back with the steel dildo in one hand and two ice packs in the other. Jutta watched with interest as he pushed the ice packs upright as far as possible into Ina's cunt. She rolled her eyes again and muffled moans came from her panties-filled slave mouth. He only left the ice packs in for a few seconds and pushed the hot dildo in instead. At the moment, the whites of her eyes bulged frighteningly large from their deep sockets. She twisted her naked body as much as she could in this strict bondage. At the same moment, Peter covered her mouth and nose with his glove so that only a loud but husky groan could be heard. Ina was in danger of fainting and Jutta, the self-confessed sadist, had already put a smelling bottle on her drinks trolley. But Ina persevered. Breathing heavily and bathed in sweat, Ina sat on three seats and was helpless at the mercy of the two flight attendants.

Peter just clamped her two cunt lobes together. For Peter it was a more mechanical process, because the dildo was supposed to heat her cunt and not slip out again.

"Here are two pillows for your back, love. Hollow back! Well, will it be soon? Your stomach shouldn't get wrinkles at your age. Yes, that's good, now there's excitement again." Jutta disappeared behind the curtain with her drinks trolley.

"We're not that mean to you. Here you have ice packs. I'll put them on your udders. But woe to them if they fall down," she warned Peter and also disappeared into the Eco.

As soon as the two of them disappeared behind the curtain to carry out their service, the machine ran into turbulence. First a slight vibration, then increasing shaking and rocking, then a bump, as if you were driving quickly on an unpaved road. Then suddenly silence. The machine glided along quietly again. But it was too late for Ina. The ice packs were on the ground.

"Jutta, look at that," Peter remarked when they had finished their service and the plane was already descending. "You want to do something good for the bitch, get her an upgrade to the business, she even has three seats to herself, even buy her ice cream because her tits are burning and this pig carelessly throws her down. Just wait!" Peter put the drinks cart down and picked up one of the ice packs from the floor. And if you didn't see, he hit the little udder with all his might and seemingly uncontrollably. Of all things, the little tit had to be used again. She was already mistreated so miserably earlier.

"That's how you make crushed ice," Peter remarked, laughing half his head.

Jutta picked up the other ice pack and pushed Peter aside. She took a more planned approach. First she gave the blows, now on the large udder, from above onto the tits, then from below, so that the udder really flew into the air and with all her might from the front onto the huge nipple. Ina whimpered. When the tit was really red and

almost turning purple, Jutta also addressed Ina's stomach and the two inner sides of her thighs with numerous hard blows.
"My little one has really red cheeks from the slaps in the face." Jutta transferred the cold of the batteries to Ina's cheeks with small, round movements. "I think we should do something about that." Ina shook her head. "Yes, yes, yes, yes, yes!", and began to let the ice accumulators land in Ina's face, first lightly and then increasingly more and more.
"Ladies and gentlemen, we are approaching Hamburg. We would now like to ask you to fasten your seat belts again, put the backrests of your seats vertically and fold up the tables in front of you. Thank you.
„Ladies and Gentlemen …"
After the announcement, Peter disappeared back into the Eco, where he had to take his designated seat. And of course he grabbed both her udders fully and brutally again and left scratch marks from his fingernails on the soles of her bare feet.
When the Airbus landed, Jutta went against the regulations and sat down with her legs spread in front of Ina's spread legs. She had brought three forks from the galley. She stuck the tines of one fork into the nipple ring of her

big tit from below. She did the same thing with the small udder. Then she turned both forks outwards and, after three-quarters of a turn, clamped both forks tightly with a tight clip that she released from her hair. With the third fork she poked Ina's clit flesh, almost absentmindedly but hard, for a while before she reached for the microphone.

"Ladies and gentlemen. Welcome to Hamburg. Please remain seated with your seat belt fastened until the machine has reached its final parking position and the seat belt signs above you have gone out. Captain Nudemus and his crew say goodbye to you here in Hamburg. We hope you enjoyed your short flight with us and we can welcome you back on board soon. Thank you and good bye."

At this announcement and the subsequent one in English, Jutta looked deeply into Ina's eyes. She thought she noticed a small smile and a barely visible nod.

"Ladies and gentlemen, your captain again. Unfortunately the front door cannot be opened. We therefore ask you to only use the rear stairs to exit the aircraft. Thank you for your understanding."

„Ladies and Gentlemen …"

AWESOME RIDE HOME

Finally the train to Hanover pulled into the platform. He was already half an hour late and Markus was already quite annoyed and exhausted from waiting in the humid evening heat. A strenuous day on patrol was behind him and all he wanted to do was go to his apartment , put his feet up and watch the Champions League game with a beer - maybe do a few sit-ups beforehand to keep his toned body fit.

The carriages at the end of the train were always pretty empty, as you had to walk the furthest at the station to get there - but Markus enjoyed the emptiness and the peace that came with it. He looked for a self-contained cabin for six people in second class. Then he ran his hand through his brown hair and picked up the daily newspaper to read. Shortly afterwards, however, the carriage door opened. 'Oh no,' he thought, looking up to see who was bothering him.

A young redhead entered the compartment and gave him a shy smile. Her skin was very pale and she had a few freckles on her face. She wore her long hair down with a mint green summer dress that pushed her breasts out a little at the top and fell loosely around her toned, slim thighs. She sat down on the seat opposite him and crossed her legs gallantly, then took a magazine out of her bag and began to leaf through it.

Markus went back to reading the daily newspaper, but he kept stealing glances at his handsome counterpart. A bead of sweat slowly trickled down her neck - no wonder, it was even hotter in the train compartment than outside. The stranger absentmindedly brushed the small drop away with her slender fingers - Markus looked at this with delighted fascination, while the young woman didn't seem to notice his gaze at all.

The train jerked along and the two of them sat in the compartment for some time. Suddenly Markus heard the woman move and looked over the edge of his newspaper -

she was placing her legs apart - she was probably sweating quite a bit in her previous position . Then he saw it: the person opposite wasn't wearing any underwear! The stranger quickly pulled the hem of the dress, which had ridden upwards, back down and looked up in shock. When she saw that she was being watched, her face turned red and she immediately glanced back at her magazine. Markus felt a tingling sensation in his pants and had to reposition himself in the seat as his cock began to get hard and required more space. He glanced at the clock: 40 minutes to his final destination - if he hurried...

In his imagination he saw the redhead in front of him, covered in light sweat, sighing and moaning. He became even harder and decided to engage the stranger in conversation.

"It's bad with this construction site, right? Delays every day!" he said.

The stranger looked up in surprise, her face still slightly flushed.

"Um, I only go on weekends when I go home from studying," she replied, "but that's true, we're actually late every time."

"What are you studying?" Markus asked.

"Law — last semester," she answered and then added with a charming smile, "At least I hope so!"

"Interesting! Then we work almost in the same business" - Markus didn't have to explain - he was wearing his uniform and since he had taken off his jacket, you could clearly see his equipment.

The stranger smiled sheepishly and looked back at her magazine. Damn.

After thinking about it for a moment, Markus tried a different technique. He left the compartment — giving the stranger a smile, which she returned — and pretended to use the restroom. When he came back, he didn't sit opposite her, but next to her.

"What's your name?" he asked blithely.

"Um, Marie Aigner. And you?"

"Mark! Nice to meet you Marie." — she smiled. "What's that on your arm? "Is that one of those Pandora bracelets?" he asked.

"Yes, exactly, I got that from my parents when I came of age last year," she replied.

"Can I take a look at this? My sister absolutely loves these pieces."

Markus held out his left hand, palm up. With his right hand he reached for his hip and with

a quiet click he removed the handcuffs that were attached there.
Marie put her hand in his to show him the jewelry in more detail - then he acted so quickly that she couldn't react at all. A handcuff snapped shut and stood up, grabbing her other wrist and locking that too with a cold, metallic click.
"What…?" asked Marie, puzzled. That's why she caught the first bell.
"Shut up, no questions!" Markus snapped at her.
"But what…" she began again and received the second resounding slap in the face. That seemed to seal her mouth.
He grabbed her upper arms and pulled her out of the seat, then pushed her down.
"Kneel down!" he ordered her and her feet gave in to his pressure.
"You're going to blow me now, got it? And if you play any tricks, there will be a big bang!" He took his semi-hard cock out of his pants and stuck it in her face. Out of sheer shock, she just knelt there and looked at him with wide eyes. The expression on his face was heavenly and turned him on even more. As she continued to remain rigid and unsettled, there was another slap as he slapped her

cheek with the palm of his hand. She gave a small cry, which he took advantage of at the same time.

He grabbed her head and buried his hands in her thick hair. Her mouth was still slightly open from her scream and so he pushed his cock directly between her lips. She tried to pull her head away, but he held her tightly and withdrew slightly from her mouth before immediately thrusting again.

Her warm lips wrapped around his shaft and his pumping movements created a suction that wanted to draw the juice out of his penis. His movements became faster and rougher, he noticed that Marie was starting to choke, but he ignored it.

The muscles in his ass clenched and he tilted his head back, feeling himself unable to hold back his cum anymore, and shot it all down her throat, tightening his grip on her hair so that she couldn't escape his feeding.

At first she didn't want to swallow, but as more and more of his semen entered her, she couldn't help but take in his cream.

When he was finished, he released his grip and said, "Good girl, now get up." She obeyed him and he helped her get up by grabbing her arm and pulling her up. Then he

took out a second pair of handcuffs from his
pocket - always careful to block her way to
the door - better safe than sorry!
"Put your hands up," he ordered her.
She seemed so scared that she obeyed him -
he adjusted her arms and secured her to the
luggage rack with the second pair of
handcuffs
Then he looked at her with satisfaction.
"What's that supposed to mean?" she asked
in a trembling voice.
The next blow hit her on her ass, causing her
to whimper.
"Shut up, you piece of shit!" he ordered her.
He ran his hand over her thighs - her skin
was soft and smooth and slightly damp from
the sultry heat. Then he stroked the dress
and her round tits. They were neither too big
nor too small and were as soft as only real
breasts could be. He briefly felt her nipples
harden and took the opportunity to take one
of them between his fingers and pinch it.
Marie moaned softly, probably in pain.
He rolled the nipple between his fingers and
squeezed briefly every now and then. After a
while he stopped playing and turned back to
her thighs. He stroked up the inside and
pushed the dress aside. Before he even

arrived at his destination, he knew what he would find. But he was shocked to find that the pretty slut was not just wet, but wet! Things couldn't have gone any better. He refrained from commenting and traced the stranger's slit with his index finger without penetrating her too deeply. Then he pressed on her clit and began to rub it under the pressure.

The redhead's hips moved and he heard her whimper. "Do you like it?" he asked, but didn't get an answer - he didn't need one. While he worked her clit with his thumb, he penetrated her with his index finger. She was velvety soft and tight, but against a little pressure from his finger, her muscles gave in willingly. After a while he pushed his middle finger and ring finger into her and let go of her clitoris so he could work her cunt better. She was twitching more and more wildly and he noticed that she was close to coming. He suddenly pulled his hand out of her. She made a disappointed noise.

"Don't worry, bitch - you're about to get something even harder!" he promised her and released his gun from the holder on his belt. When Marie saw what Markus was planning to do, she begged him: "Oh no, please don't! Please don't!" she whimpered, but with a few well-aimed slaps on her bottom he quieted her. "Shut your dirty mouth! "No one can hear you here anyway," he snapped. He checked whether the weapon was secured and took out all the cartridges to be on the safe side.

Then he ran the cold shaft of the gun over her wet cunt and rubbed the piece with her pussy juice so that it would slide better into her. At the same time, he took her swollen clit between his thumb and forefinger and rubbed it with gentle pressure.

Marie seemed to completely forget what he was about to penetrate her with. He positioned the gun and pushed the hard, cold metal into her wet pussy. Her previous whimpers now turned into her first real moans. She didn't seem like a woman who was screaming with pleasure, but Markus found her sounds more than erotic.

He pulled the pistol almost completely out again and then pushed it even deeper into Marie's cunt. He repeated his thrusts and each time the metal of the weapon became more and more coated with her cunt juice.

When he realized that Marie was close to cumming again, he stopped his movements

and left the weapon buried deep inside her. Maybe he wouldn't let her come today! The thought of her remaining unsatisfied on the edge of orgasm turned him on.
He walked around her and lifted her dress - then slapped her ass with the palm of his hand while the hard shaft of the gun remained stuck in her cunt. She moans. He struck again and watched as the weapon moved inside her.
Every now and then he switched from one butt cheek to the other and only stopped when her bottom was evenly colored red. Time for him to have a little fun himself before the train would reach its station.
He pulled the gun out of Marie and her pussy juice dripped onto the floor of the compartment. The horny pig was totally excited.
Without further ado, he put the weapon in his bag - he would probably have to clean it more than thoroughly this evening, but this fuck was more than worth it to him!
He then grabbed Marie's legs between the backs of her knees and rested them on the crooks of his arms - her wet pussy was positioned directly in front of his throbbing cock, which was still protruding from his

unzipped pants. It was a really cool sight to see her hanging in the air with her tied arms - he could easily penetrate her because her pussy was so eager to be filled.

He fucked her, which wasn't easy as the train continued to jerk along. The whole foreplay had made him pretty horny and he came after a short time. He would have liked to treat her breasts with his hands, but in this position he literally had his hands full.

Besides, Marie might have come faster than he did - and he didn't want to give her the reward of an orgasm.

So he came quickly and hard and pumped all his cum into her without Marie having time to cum. He then pulled out of her and placed her legs on the floor. But these gave way and so Marie hung weakly from their attachment to the luggage rack.

Markus was extremely satisfied and put his cock in his pants. His station was announced over the loudspeaker. Perfect timing!

He carefully released Marie from the handcuffs, but she could not stand on her shaky legs and sank to her knees in front of him - an indescribable sight.

He packed his utensils into his bag and picked up his uniform jacket when a train conductor opened the compartment door. He blushed slightly as he realized the scene before his eyes - Marie, covered in sweat, looking down at the floor and breathing heavily, kneeling on the floor with her legs apart and the smell of sex in the compartment.

A dirty smile spread across the conductor's face - the guy was in his mid-forties and a little stocky.

"Is everything okay?" he asked.

"Yes, thank you very much - I have to get out now anyway," replied Markus.

"And the lady?" the conductor continued to ask.

"Just having a little bout of weakness — maybe just check on her later — just to be sure."

The conductor cleared the door and muttered, "Oh yes, that's my duty," before disappearing down the aisle.

Markus smiled and thought: Maybe, dear Marie, you can still come today! Then the train came to a stop and Markus left the pretty redhead behind without another word.

ANOTHER LESSON

I know I'm not worth it because I'm such a horny little bitch. Nevertheless, I thank you for the lesson you taught me. As a thank you, I open your pants and take out your heavy balls. As always, your thick cock scares me a bit because it is so extremely heavy. But I obediently take your thick glans and carefully cream it with both hands.

I gently massage your hard balls again and again and tell you that I tremble at the thought that you are about to impale me and torture me with this huge strap .

But you say that I have no other choice. Now I had this lesson to learn. Your enormously thick and heavy cock is now shaking in my hands. I jerked him off hard and prepared him

nicely with lube. You order me, with a hard voice and bad words, to prepare my fuck hole now.
Although my hole is glistening with slime, I still have to rub myself with a lot of lubricant in front of you.
I think I'm ready now, but you say my little pussy is far too narrow for your thick strap and you have to make sure I'm dilated. You roughly take my lips with both hands and pull them apart.
I moan loudly. You also take my inner lips and stretch them too. Now my hole is open but you are not satisfied yet. You have pliers like a gynecologist to hold my lips wide open and now you're pushing a dildo into me that's even thicker than your shockingly thick cock. The thunderstorm within me begins.
I can't hold back and moan loudly, but you give me a hard slap in the face. I have to be quiet.
I have to apologize to you for my horniness, it's always the same with me. Because I'm so difficult to fuck and I'm not really good for it, I have to jerk your cock hard again.
I'm lying there with the big dildo in my far too tight pussy, I imagine you're getting impatient and calling me unfit for fucking. You first have

to put cream on me and dilate my pussy because I'm constantly fingering myself out of sheer horniness and constantly masturbating myself. And I couldn't stand a proper strap. Your patience has come to an end and you grab me by the dildo, which you push in and out of me excessively hard and quickly.

It's hard for me not to moan, my eyes widen enormously and I feel your cock now hardening like a rock in my hands. With a jerk you pull out the dildo and bang me so that I turn around and you can finally take me from behind. You have to tell me everything first. On all fours I raise my ass towards you, but you are only interested in my thick, juicy lips, which you now pull wide apart. And even though I just had your cock in my hand, I couldn't breathe when you pushed it mercilessly into my hole. I feel your balls hitting my clit, you're thrusting so hard. I gasp even though I know I have to keep my mouth shut, but you heard it. You push my shoulders hard onto the floor so that my ass stands even higher and you can serve yourself more comfortably. Your fucking rhythm becomes harder and faster, more and more merciless. I bite my hand and tears come out of my eyes because you are so hard today. But I have this lesson to learn if I want to be good enough for you. Finally you squirt everything into me, it's an incredible amount and I feel how your twitching never seems to end. After you pull out your cock, I have to cover myself with both hands because I already know that you can't stand it if I drool all over everything else.

I'm still shaking all over in fear of the hard violence with which you fucked me, but I've already learned that I can only move when you allow me to.
Finally you send me to the toilet to clean my pussy. You watch me very closely so that I don't touch myself unnecessarily and possibly do it myself.
But I already know that I can only have an orgasm if you allow me to do so first. When I'm clean again, you slap me because you can see that I'm still horny. Do I still not have enough? As a punishment, my hands are tied behind my back again and I have to go to bed immediately

THE SEARCH FOR THE LIMITS

We'll meet. The first time. We both just want one thing. Sex! Pure lust, lust! Getting to know our limits .
You picked me up at the train station and organized everything. A room in a hotel.
We're going into town first. It's early evening. We're going to eat something. Let's talk first, we don't know each other. But we don't stay there for long, we're restless and want to know.
We drive to the hotel, get the room key and go up. Top floor, it's empty there at this time of year, we are the only guests there.
The room has a large bed, a bathroom with a tub and shower. We don't need any more.

You close the door behind me. Come towards me, throw me on the bed. You pull up your skirt and tear down your panties.

We're already horny, we don't need any initiation. You throw yourself on me and take me. Just take the time to unzip your pants, nothing more. I want to protest, but you close my mouth with an almost brutal kiss. I can only moan. I feel your cock entering me hard and fast. And so you continue, hard and fast. It's awesome. Without discussion, without questions. Just like that.

My moans get louder. I hear your panting in my right ear. You don't kiss me anymore, you just thrust as hard and as hard as you can. I feel a tingling sensation in my abdomen that quickly gets stronger.

You also feel a pulsation in your cock. Our moans become louder, almost ending in a scream, right at the moment you pour yourself into me. Exhausted, we fall into each other's arms. Stay lying down for now. Gain new strength. The night is still long and still lies ahead of us.

We start caressing each other, undressing and slowly exploring each other's bodies. It's almost tender. Do we want that? No, not actually. We want more. We both want to test our limits.

Our movements become faster, firmer. You don't caress my breast anymore, you massage it. Pinch me in. Careful but firm. I groan.

I have to go to the toilet, let me go.

I get up and go to the bathroom. As soon as I'm done, the door opens and you come in. You bend me with my upper body over the edge of the tub. You're holding me there with your left hand. With your right hand you reach between my legs. You rub my clit, you keep pulling on my ring. With two fingers you slide into my pussy. She's all wet. With my wetness on your fingers you stroke over my perineum, up to my bottom. You rub the moisture there. You repeat the whole thing, twice, three times… Not without increasing the pressure of your finger on my bottom each time. I groan. I know what you want. I'm afraid. It hurts. But you won't let me go. You're holding me over the tub. I feel your finger in my butt. Notice how horny it makes you, the thought of penetrating me there. Feeling my tightness there. You stick a second finger in your bottom. Very carefully. Move your fingers inside me. Trying to stretch me enough so you can put your cock in it. The feeling is awesome. Crazy!

I notice how difficult it is for you to control yourself. Your breathing also quickens. Suddenly you're behind me. Your hands are gripping my pelvis. I feel the tip of your cock on my bottom. How he carefully tries to penetrate me. My fear is back. You feel it.

The moment you penetrate me with a powerful thrust, you slap my ass firmly with the palm of your hand. It really bangs. I forgot to tense up because of the shock. I am amazed to feel that your cock is completely inside me. You stay quiet for a little moment. But only to then thrust even harder.

I scream. Not from pain, from pure lust. Your moans also become louder. This tightness has you completely under control. Your cock under control. You thrust, hard and unstoppable. I don't want to stop you at all. What you do makes me horny. My abdomen is on fire, my pussy is on fire.

I feel that I'm coming. Yessssssssssssssss. I shout it out. You keep thrusting. I can only moan. You also notice that you are not far away from your orgasm.

You pause. Don't want to come yet. Pull your cock out of my butt and push it into my pussy.

And keeps thrusting. I'm getting horny again.
The feeling of your cock in my pussy, your
loud moans...
I notice how it arises within me again, this
feeling. You keep fucking me mercilessly.
Drive us to orgasm together.
Sweaty, we gasp for breath. I climb into the
bathtub, sit down there and want to take a
quick shower. You come to me in the tub. You
stand in front of me and just say you really
need to pee. You look at me expectantly.
What do you want from me?
You start stroking me again. I'm immediately
on fire again. I'm immediately horny again, as
if there had been no break. No orgasm. You
touch my pussy again. Rub my clit until I start
moaning again. Suddenly, when I don't think I
can take it anymore, you sit up. You put
yourself above me. You take your cock in
your hand, point it at me……and pee on me.
On my neck, my chest, between my legs. At
first I'm horrified. What are you doing? But
the feeling, the jet directed at me, the warmth
of your urine. I don't know how it happened.
Can't explain it to myself. But it was enough.
That alone was enough for me to cum again.
We let water run into the tub. A relaxing bath
is exactly what we need right now. I quickly

run into the room and come back with a bottle of champagne and two glasses. We make ourselves comfortable in the tub. Drink the champagne and talk about what you just experienced.

When the water starts to get cold, we get out of the tub, dry ourselves with the hotel's thick and fluffy towels and go back into the room. Satisfied, we collapse onto the bed.

We hug each other tenderly. Start cuddling. Yes, there is something tender, familiar between us.

Our borders can remain stolen from us for today, they don't interest us at the moment. We want tenderness. Both.

You lean over me. Start kissing me tenderly. My face, you play with your tongue in my ears. It tickles, but it feels good. I shudder. I start to caress you. Your arms, your chest. And kiss you. My tongue plays with your nipples. They straighten up and become stiff. I keep kissing you, all the way to your cock. Stick out my tongue and circle your glans. Again and again. I close my lips around your cock and take it deep into my mouth. Start sucking on him. You taste good. I take it in my hand at the same time. While I lick your

glans, I jerk it off with my right hand. He's already grown up. And hard.
You grab my pussy with one hand and start fingering me. I'm already wet with anticipation. You carefully insert two fingers into my pussy. Move those in me. You want to lick me too, lie on top of me. Your cock is in my mouth. You gently lick my crack with your tongue. Once, twice……Each time you try to push it a little deeper into me. It's an awesome feeling! Makes me really hot. Every time your tongue strokes my clit I cringe.
You go down and kneel between my legs. You look at my pussy, caress it. You notice how excited I am when you touch my clit and you take advantage of that. I writhe under you, under your touch. My moans get louder.
You lie on top of me, your cock strokes through my crack. I feel him slowly sliding into me. Very slowly and tenderly. Then you move inside me. Very tenderly. Your moans get louder. I follow your movements. Very slowly we come to orgasm at the same time. It is wonderful. Nothing can eliminate tenderness. Or is it?
I don't know it. We'll see more tomorrow. Now we just want to cuddle together. Enjoy what you experienced.

We fall asleep tightly hugged. We still have a whole weekend ahead of us. Will we still find our limits?
Certainly

SUBLERA'S NIGHTMARE

This is what you get from going on blind dates ; I thought to myself. I couldn't say it. Because the guy had shoved a gag between my jaws and tied it tightly behind my head. At least the lacing doesn't pinch, I thought ironically. He kindly pulled your mask over my head beforehand, leaving only my eyes and mouth exposed. So far everything had gone quite well and as we had agreed. I lay tightly wrapped in foil in front of him. Unable to move and with a mask over my head. However, the gag was not agreed upon and that caused me to; Given my current position , I have a few concerns. I didn't know the guy any further. Good; we had fucked a few times and he fists really well. He also has a nice, natural, dominant streak. And that just makes me really hot...

I saw him grab a large enema syringe from the cupboard behind him. That was new. So far during our <u>sessions</u> he had enjoyed himself by pushing his fist and various dildos and plugs into my cunt. I'm actually not that into <u>enemas</u> . This type of loss of control is not what I mean when I think of <u>submissive</u> and passive. But I couldn't make that clear to him anymore. All that came out of my mouth was grumbling and it had wrapped my body really well today. A whole roll of cling film had gone on it. And I was completely unable to move as a result. I couldn't even think about sliding back and forth.

I was told. I'm not sure whether it was the thought of the enema or the built-up heat under the foil. Anyway, he took the enema syringe out of the cupboard, went into the bathroom with it and I heard hissing, clattering and finally a smacking noise. Apparently he was filling the enema.

We once chatted about his fantasies in this direction and I made it clear to him that this wasn't my thing. After that it was no longer an issue between us. Until now. I tried to calm myself and get my heart rate under control by saying to myself: what's going to happen? Your cunt is rinsed clean. You are well

stretched and can tolerate a lot of water. At least that's what I knew from my own experiments in the tub. *smile*
I saw him come out of the bathroom, somewhat calm again. In one hand the large enema and in the other a five-liter plastic canister in which liquid of an indefinable color was sloshing.
He came over to me and turned me onto my stomach. Now I can only see him out of the corner of my eye. But that was more than enough. Somehow I was glad that he hadn't given me a blindfold in addition to the gag. How little you can be happy with...
I thought briefly about how he was going to insert the enema into me, because after all, my ass was wrapped just as tightly as the rest of my body. And my cunt was inaccessible. As if he had heard my thoughts, I saw a dirty grin on his face. "Hold still bitch. I'm now going to slit the foil over your cunt and we don't want any blood to flow…"
Kind. Really nice. So what else could I do but lie still? I heard a soft squeak and felt a cool draft on my cunt, which was immediately replaced by a thumb that pushed itself roughly into my cunt. "Well, you love that, you bitch. - Yes; Just whimper a little." With these

words he pushed two more fingers into my cunt. Normally this isn't a challenge for me, but due to the tightly pressed ass cheeks and the tied thighs; which were firmly fixed by the film, it was a completely different feeling...

As quickly as his fingers were inside me, he withdrew them and applied the tip of the enema. He must have lubricated it properly because it slipped into me without any significant resistance. A little gentle pressure was enough and my asshole opened. Shortly afterwards I felt a slight pressure inside me and heard a smacking sound as he emptied the enema inside me. And I heard his breathing getting a little quicker. It seemed to make him horny. My cock also stirred, but only had the opportunity to grow imperceptibly in the narrow prison that the foil represented. And so my horniness caused me more pain than pleasure.

He said something to me that I didn't understand. But I wasn't able to make that clear to him because of the gag. He probably interpreted my hmmpf as agreement. Because the next thing I heard was: "All right, bitch, then you're about to get your second load." But close your ass nicely so that nothing leaks out."

Great, how am I supposed to do that? But I tried really hard to keep my cunt stuck to the enema as he slowly pulled it out. And then flexing your ass. It went quite well. At least as far as I can tell. I couldn't see anything. And you hardly feel anything. This foil everywhere. Interesting how perception changes...

I was still thinking, but he had probably already finished the second load, as he put it. The enema pressed itself into my cunt again. This time completely without resistance. Smack and the thing was in. He had apparently touched j-lube. So that was in the canister. But why so much? Surely he wouldn't want to push everything into me? He couldn't possibly try that. I felt heat and slight panic rise within me again. I wasn't capable of any other reaction anyway, so I tried to calm myself down. With doubtful success. Her second load was already pushing quite well. Impossible to keep my cunt closed when he pulls out the enema now, I thought. But he had probably expected that. The enema out and a plug in was almost one. Oh, it's small, hopefully the plug will hold, I thought as I felt it... until the part inside me got bigger. This bastard. I once told him in a chat that I didn't like these inflatable parts.

I was panting heavily and drooling past the gag. He didn't seem to hear my grumbling, or just didn't care. Probably the latter.

My stomach was now clearly pressing against the foil and against the bed. After all, I was lying on it too! The slap on my ass that he gave me encouragingly only made things worse.

"Now let's see what else fits in there," I heard his voice.

Even more? I already felt like I was four months pregnant. Everything in me screamed to get rid of the plug and ease my bowels. He let a little air out of the plug, pulled it out and almost immediately replaced it with the enema, which he pushed into me all the way. At least that's how it felt. And then the next push came. My stomach bulged even more and I felt like my insides were bulging. At the same time, I felt some of the stuff he was pushing into me find its way past the enema and wobble out of my cunt.

He quickly pulled out the enema again and just as quickly stuffed the plug in to pump it up energetically. Even further than last time, it seemed to me. Because this time I had the feeling that my rosette was being ripped open from the inside. But the plug was stuck, preventing the stuffing from leaving my insides. By now I was moaning uncontrollably into the gag. I felt sick and felt like I was going to pass out. I felt myself being shaken by severe abdominal pain. I barely noticed my surroundings anymore. I just wanted it to be over.

I simply had to look grotesque: in foil; with mask and gag. This huge thing in the cunt and the stomach bloated. I continued to be wracked with violent spasms as he pumped the rubber plug into my stretched sphincter thicker and thicker. I really shouldn't have told him about my rape fantasy, it occurred to me briefly. But that thought was immediately drowned out by the pain that seemed to flood my entire abdomen. All I could do was whimper and whine softly. I was no longer able to think clearly. I was just riding a wave of pain and the cramps didn't seem to want to stop. My body twitched uncontrollably in a way I had only ever experienced during an electro session.

In my twilight state, I didn't really feel how he let the air out of the plug and how it shot out

of me. Followed by a gush of j-lube, because that's what the bastard had pumped into me. The next thing I knew, I was lying in this j-lube mud that had just been inside me. The stuff spread across the foil, in the foil and just seemed to be everywhere below my stomach.
I heard him grunt with pleasure as he slid onto me and he sank his cock into my cunt and began to fuck me. After the pressure I had just endured, I was really grateful for it. And at that moment I would have really done anything he would have asked of me.
Fortunately, it seemed to be enough for him to have fun in and on me.
My cunt offered no resistance and the rest of my body didn't seem to belong to me anymore anyway...

THE OLD MAN

I was just 19 back then and still quite sporty, unlike today. At 178 I had 85kg and not a trace of a stomach. The reason for this was actually that I was working as an electrician and antenna builder in Cologne. Up the stairs, down the stairs… every day. I also did a few things for good friends outside of work. When I got home my mother was waiting for me. "Listen son, Mrs. Müller across the street asked if you could connect a new stove to her father's house? You should call her!". I nodded, took the piece of paper and called the old lady. Her father, 75, has a new stove and it needs to be installed and connected. That would be worth 50 marks to her. I agreed and asked for the address.
The next evening I drove straight from work to the gentleman's house. I rang the bell and the door opened. Standing in front of me was a slim, older man in a gray suit, a little taller than me, his hair neatly combed back. Everything about him seemed very accurate.

He greeted me very politely. I felt a little strange in my short cut-off jeans and baggy T-shirt.

We went into the kitchen where he immediately offered me something to drink. I gratefully took the water and drank it in one gulp. He smiled warmly and poured more water. Nice grandpa !

Then I started work. First the old stove had to come out, which was quite a bit of fiddling. Oh crap, the cable was rigid and had to be replaced. But it wasn't that easy because it disappeared behind the sink. Crap, crap, crap, I thought and started emptying the sink. The can was there. It was really difficult, so I lay on my back like a car mechanic and tinkered with the can. I cursed under my breath. The old man knelt down next to me and rested his hand on my thigh... quite high up, I winced and hit my head. "Oh young man, have you done something to yourself... can I help?" he asked kindly. He leaned forward a little more and his hand slipped a little higher. There was revolution in my pants. My little one wanted out... it had been a long time since he last had sex.

"No, everything's ok... it's just a bit stupid here," I replied, "but maybe you could hold the lamp and shine it on the can?" He reached for the flashlight he held out and shone it into the closet. His hand slid higher again and was now right on my balls. I would burst at any moment, the jeans had a huge bulge. And was that really just an oversight? No idea. I looked at him from under the sink, but he had an innocent face. Definitely an oversight.

20 minutes later I was finally finished. My shirt was completely soaked with sweat when I was finally able to push the stove into the cupboard. He stood next to me and watched my work. I smiled kindly at him. "Almost done" Then I screwed the stove onto the cupboard. When I wanted to tighten the last screw, it fell off and I had to fumble it back out between the stove flap and the stove. I bent down to do this. And then it happened, his hand could clearly be felt on my ass . He rubbed my ass and I thought it was nice, but took a little longer than necessary. As if nothing had happened, I tightened the last screw, his hand remained on my ass. I finished the work with a loud "so!"

When I turned to him, I could see a bulge in his suit pants and his cheeks were flushed. I took my voltage tester and checked again,

turned the stove on to see if it got hot...
everything was ok.
"So Mr. Schmitz, everything is ok again.
"Stove works… can you cook again" I said.
He smiled gratefully. "Can I offer you a beer
now, young man. And if I'm honest, it would
be nice if they stayed a little longer. As you
get older, you're always quickly alone." I
nodded. "You're welcome, Mr. Schmitz, I
have time today!" He took two bottles of beer
from the fridge and walked ahead of me into
the living room. Everything was old but
tasteful. I also wanted to know what else the
old man had come up with. You could tell
from his pants that he was still horny.
He put glasses on the table and poured from
the bottles. Then he sat down next to me and
we toasted each other. I was still sweating
like a horse and wiped my face with my shirt.
He stared at my exposed stomach and licked
his lips with his tongue. Then he took off his
jacket and undid the top button. I sat right
next to him and we chatted about old times.
He really had a lot to tell and they were funny
stories that made us both laugh . At some
point he put his hand on my thigh again. I
acted as if I didn't notice anything. He started
to crawl my leg with his fingertips. I was

already horny anyway… Man oh man. He very carefully pushed his hand up a little further. I continued to chatter and talk to him. There was a sparkle in his eyes.
Now his hand reached my thick cock bulge. "Mr Schmitz, what are you doing there?" I asked. Startled, he withdrew his hand, but I caught it and placed it directly on my packed cock. "Why stop… I like it" I said to him smiling. Now he became brave. He turned to me and massaged the denim with his whole hand. You could tell he liked it. "Hmm, wait a minute, Mr. Schmitz. I'll make the whole thing a little easier. I think that's in your interest," I said to him. Then I stood up and took off my jeans and my shirt. He looked a little surprised, but also very lustful.
I sat down next to him again and pulled one leg up a little. He hesitated for a moment, then boldly grabbed my bag again. You could see that I had a massive boner under my panties. He contented himself with caressing my balls for a while. His hand was shaking slightly with excitement. Then all of a sudden he reached through the trouser leg into my panties. I groaned. He now had the shaft firmly in his fist and was jerking me off... slowly and with pleasure. This couldn't last

long and I also took off my panties. He was excited and asked me to come and stand in front of him. No sooner said than done, I stood naked in front of him. By now he had opened his fly and pulled out his big old cock. He stood half-stiff in the doorway. He caressed my body with his hands and pinched my nipples . Then he focused on my cock again. He jerked it and kneaded my balls. Then he grabbed my ass cheeks with both hands and pulled me towards him. He looked up at me and then he took my boner in his mouth. I groaned and pinched my own nipples. I pushed my ass forward towards him. And at first he just sucked, then pushed my foreskin back with his lips and then sucked the glans. I didn't think such an old gentleman could suck like that. He became more and more stormy and sucked the cock deep into his mouth. He was able to swallow it all the way without gagging.

His fingertips played with my asshole. Now he grabbed my pelvis and pulled me around. Then he gently pushed me forward and I supported myself on the living room table. He placed his large hands on my cheeks and kneaded them. Then he pushed his legs a little to the side. I obediently did what my

hands commanded. "What a hot ass my boy... before now I would have banged you hard and fucked the shit out of you!" he said. It's great to hear him talk like that, such a distinguished man. "I'm going to lick your cunt now, you little pig" came next and you could immediately feel his tongue circling around my hole. His hands pulled my ass apart. He licked and sucked and I moaned in pleasure. Every now and then he pulled my cock hard behind me and licked it. It went on like this for a little while, my legs were about to give in, I was so horny.
The pressure was evident as he pushed his finger into my ass. He fucked me with it and I obeyed. With the fingers of his left hand he had formed a ring around my balls and was pulling them down hard. I enjoyed it. My God, Grandpa was horny… a pig before the Lord. I had now laid my head on the cold table, my ass was sticking up towards him. I wished so much that he would just fuck me hard. He pulled his finger out of my intestines and shortly afterwards did something else. It was thicker and hard. Very slowly he pushed the thing through my sphincter. I moaned and whimpered... it hurt, but it was also horny. It was dripping down from my cock. "I knew

your asshole could take more than a finger. Come on you horny pig, push it!" I did as I was told and whatever it was slipped into my ass.
He was satisfied and pushed it back and forth... fucking my hole with it. "So you little cunt, turn around, kneel down and suck my cock!" I obediently followed this order. I turned around. His face glowed and his eyes sparkled greedily.
I fell to my knees, the part in my ass hurt and made me even weaker. He scooted forward on the sofa and undid the belt and button. Then he lifted his ass and let me take off his pants. He spread his legs and his cock stood half-stiff from a bush of gray hair. "Come on, mare, suck!" this command wouldn't have been necessary. I put my arms on his thighs and licked the really huge thing. There were more than 20 cm and a really enormous size to digest. I pushed back the foreskin and took him into my mouth. His taste was amazing, distinctly like piss and sweat. He groaned pleasantly. I started sucking his cock as ordered. My mouth was almost filled with the cock. He slid down a little further and spread his legs very wide, he didn't think such an old man could do that.

"Now, cunt, you first lick my hole and don't forget the balls!" another instruction. I ducked lower and saw the asshole that was slightly open. Again I began obediently to carry out his orders. I licked the hole and then started sucking. He liked that. He stroked my head and babbled obscenities. My tongue was able to slide a long way into his intestines, the sphincter hardly offered any resistance. I licked, sucked and sucked and heard him hoot enthusiastically. To make things even better, I had his cock firmly in my right hand and was jerking him off. His hole twitched... when I wanted to put my finger in he shouted at me, "Hello cunt, you're the hot gay bitch here and you're going to get fucked. You have to serve me... so stay away!" I thought what a shame and sucked on the long hanging balls. I love old sacks when they hang beautifully.

Then the hole again... then the balls again. I licked as if there was nothing else left. It went on like this for a while, he stroked my hair and grunted with pleasure. Then he pulled me up "Come on...swallow!". His cock disappeared into my mouth again. I sucked him hard and he was a little harder, but it probably wouldn't be enough to fuck. I fucked him with my lips and suddenly he pushed my head down. The cock slipped down my throat, way too deep and I had to gag. Then he let go again and repeated the game again a short time later.

I gagged and saliva flowed in streams. This happened to me several times and I thought I was going to puke. At some point he stopped. "Soo, now finish it, and remember, swallow well!" I nodded with his cock in my mouth. And started sucking like crazy. His moans became louder and louder, repeatedly interrupted by yes... yes... yes... shouts. I sucked obsessively and thought it wouldn't work. Then the time had come. He shot it... and how, thick and creamy it shot out. A large amount that I couldn't get down quickly enough with the thing still squirting in my mouth. He held my head and pressed it on his cock... and he roared like a stabbed animal. I thought I was choking on the juice and wasn't able to keep it all down, some of it ran out of the corners of my mouth. After 4-5 spurts he was finally finished… and I just thought thank God!

Of course I had to lick it clean, but that was really the smallest problem. I felt like my throat was sore and I had eaten too much. I burped and it tasted like cum... bull cum! He sat on the sofa and smiled happily and contentedly. Exhausted, I sat down on the sofa and noticed the thing in my ass again. I had to stand in front of him again, bend over and he tore it out of my cunt with a jerk, amidst my scream. Of course I had to lick it clean in front of him. It was a self-made wooden plug because good Mr. Schmitz used to be a carpenter and made quite a few of them. He gave it to me. Half an hour later I was back in my car, enriched by a few experiences, 150 DM and a wooden plug. The rest of the evening I had to regurgitate his sperm again and again... well... and grin every time. When I went to bed I jerked off and squirted myself in the face... oh yeah... there was a piece of wood stuck in my ass

THE KEGEL EVENING

You and I have been together for a few months. One day you ask me if I would like to have a bowling evening with you and your friends. Of course I happily agree. A little later we all sit together at a large wooden table in the bowling alley. I'll sit next to you, snuggled up close, while you talk to your friends. While I pretend to listen intently, the only thing I can think about is your hot cock. Without hesitation, I stroke your crotch gently and unnoticed. You don't look at me, but I notice how horny it makes you. So while you continue to chat with your friends, I open your fly and slide my little hand into your pants. Through my underwear, I start rubbing your cock slowly but hard. You're obviously uncomfortable with me jerking you off in front of your friends. Now the person in front of you stands up. So this is ready, you quickly take my hand out of your pants and walk forward. Nobody but me saw your bulge in your pants and I have to smile slightly . When you come back and quickly sit down next to me again, I whisper in your ear how wet, no, how wet I am. I get up and walk towards the toilet. When I look back at the table briefly, I see you get up and follow me. I start to grin and quickly check to see if anyone else is in the toilet, I quickly pull you into a stall and immediately start kissing you wildly. You push me against the wall and knead my tight little ass while I give you a long-lasting French kiss. When you start kissing my neck, I'm overwhelmed and I have a strong orgasm. I grab my hand in your messy hair and push you to your knees. You immediately understand what I want from you and pull down my leggings including the thong and immediately bury your face between my legs. I feel your tongue running through my crack and dancing around my clit. Moaning loudly, I push your head even deeper between my legs. You now fuck my tight hole with your tongue and literally suck the juice out of my pussy. I get 2 more orgasms before I push you away and stand in front of you with wobbly legs. But now you also want to be satisfied and are looking at me demandingly. I understand you and skillfully open your pants and pull them down along with your underwear. Your half-stiff cock jumps out at me and I take it in my small hand. Even when semi-stiff, it is at least 16 centimeters tall. When I see your cock in front of me, my pussy heats up even more. I quickly take it into my mouth and lick the drops of pleasure from your glans. I'm starting slowlysuck and jerk your cock on the side. At some point I'll take it all in my mouth and let you take control. You take my two pigtails in your hand and slowly start to fuck my mouth. As I feel your cock getting longer and harder, I start to finger myself with my index and middle fingers and rub my clit with my thumb. Meanwhile you're constantly ramming your cock down my throat and using me like a sex doll. I feel your cock start to twitch and I immediately know what that means. I quickly escape your grasp. After all, I still want to have fun. So I stand up, turn around and lean forward towards the door. Without waiting long, you unexpectedly ram your cock all the way into me. I squeak briefly and jerk forward. You stay inside me for a moment to get used to my tight pussy and then start moving quickly

MY FIRST ASS FUCK

He was a force - but he was far too much of a gentleman to seduce me on the many evenings we spent together. I didn't dare either, I thought a girl wouldn't do that.
... I think I'm the prettiest in our company, out of about 300 women. With my 1.60 height, my dark complexion and my toned body, my small apple breasts and my hard bubble butt, I attract men's attention.
At some point the guy, named Tom, turned away from me... and ended up with the second nicest person in the company. So I came up with a ruse... I don't know what the other woman has to offer sexually - I wanted to do everything...
So I invited him to my house under an excuse and first discussed a serious professional topic with him.
Then I went into the bathroom, took off my clothes and sat doggy style in front of the tub.

A few days earlier I had bought the lubricant "Slick and Slide" for my bottom , which I then dripped onto my middle finger and slowly pushed it through the outer sphincter of my bottom.
A loud moan escaped me as I hit the inner ring of hard muscle...
I thought Tom should drill it out - and so I called him...
He opened the ajar door and looked at my bottom, with my middle finger stuck in its oily rosette, and stopped dead in his tracks.
I said; "I want you to fuck my ass". I don't normally talk like that, but I heard it like that in a porn movie and I think it turns men on. And right...
...He took off his clothes and I saw his boner sticking up - my God, I thought, it's way too big for my little butthole.
He gently pulled my finger out of my butt and took the bottle of lubricant and a towel. He gently cleaned my asshole dry, then flicked his tongue around the rear pleasure entrance and then, pulling my cheeks apart firmly, pushed it in - that was cool...
Then finally he put his oiled finger on my asshole and pressed it until the first resistance. While he teased my clitoris with

his other hand, he waited until the inner gate opened ever so slightly. Now he drove slowly - millimeter by millimeter into my intestinal canal and kept dripping some of the oil into my ass opening. I felt the oil seeping into my intestines and wetting me deep inside me, felt his finger stroking the inner wall of my intestines and making me more and more supple, felt him suddenly press a second finger into the narrow opening and reach my first hot anal orgasm, which I assumed didn't even exist.

He slowly pulled his two fingers out of my tight hole and placed his throbbing hard boner on the asshole. When his glans penetrated, I thought I was getting a tennis ball pushed in and I screamed - I panicked - I wanted to allow everything, but not this one Huge boner in my ass... it would tear me apart.

But Tom wasn't deterred - he stayed in that position and only pushed forward when I also relaxed the inner ring. Slowly he slid deeper - I could now feel him in my intestines deeper than any finger could have penetrated, but his journey into my core was not yet over I tried to slide forward - he was too much for me - but there was the tub - so I tensed my

sphincter - tried to force his huge cock out of me, but I achieved the exact opposite - he groaned with pleasure and his cock was still growing
continued on and pushed further into my ass canal….
The initial incredible stretching pain gave way to budding pleasure - this feeling of being filled to the point of bursting, this friction to depths that I had never even imagined in my dreams and the feelings that it created couldn't even be compared to a vaginal fuck I had an incredible orgasm. When he was up to his balls in my asshole, he rotated his pelvis and hit my G-spot with the hard tip of his cock and gently rubbed my clitoris with his hand, reaching under my stomach. My pleasure juice squirted out of my clam and I had the most violent climax I had ever known. Then I heard him say: "Now it's my turn" and I thought he was going to unload hotly inside me - no - he pulled his hard cock back until only the glans was stretching my bottom and pushed in again - pulled it back and pushed back in and plowed my ass and fucked and fucked..
I prayed that he would finally come now, but he said: "Give me a little more time…" and

now pulled his boner completely out of me. I noticed how my dilated asshole immediately began to contract again, but as soon as it was closed, he squeezed your tube again through the tight ring, slid all the way into my intestines and then pulled it out completely again. He watched again as my intestinal canal closed so that he could drive his boner all the way into me again. This way he fucked me again
and climaxed again, then he became faster, his breath flew, his tube began to twitch inside me and I thought, he won't inject into my intestines just yet, when I felt the first jet of his hot lava deep inside my intestines shot, followed by countless more discharges..
He collapsed on top of me and simply left his tube in my ass and I now tightened my asshole violently, relaxed it again and wanted to milk him like that. His cock hardened again and he fucked my tight ass crater again like a man possessed until he squirted once more deep into my intestines. Then he showered and walked away without a word. For the next few days my bottom felt like it had been bruised - sitting down was out of the question. I hope he still dreams today of what I allowed back then to win him over.

AWESOME HOTEL STAY

… it was already 10 p.m. when I arrived at the hotel.
So this time Joe was happy about the offer that the pretty, blonde girl at the reception made to him that he could still eat in the hotel restaurant if he wanted, and she would let the kitchen know.
She had made the offer to this regular guest so many times, but so far he had refused every time. Each time she looked disappointed. He had been a regular guest at her parents ' hotel for two years and she had long wanted to eat him out one day. She had already raved about him to a waitress with whom she had been working and living at the hotel, and so they had an agreement. Nilüfer, the waitress, was supposed to get the guest excited and then when she managed to get

into his room, she was supposed to let her know and she would join them.

He freshened up quickly and rushed into the restaurant, looked around and realized that he was the only customer.

A petite, southern beauty, fawn-colored skin, black eyes and equally black hair, in a classic waitress costume, greeted him with a radiant smile. "I've been waiting for you, here's the card. Would you like to look inside first or can I get you something to drink?"

"Wow," she thought, "that's cute – now I understand Beate, I want that too…"

She had been living in a small room in the next building in this training hotel, which was affiliated with a renowned hotel management school, for two years and was longing to finally have sex again. The owners' daughter, Beate, had just let them in on their plan. They were really very close friends, she had introduced Beate, even though she was eight years older than her 20s, to the secrets of love between women and enjoyed their hours together in which they caressed each other and used love toys inserted all body openings and always experienced huge climaxes. She loved Beate's womanly body, her large, firm breasts, her narrow waist and her round

apple bottom . Since they were both almost the same height, Beate was clearly more woman than she was.
But apparently the guest still seemed to have taken a liking to her, because the sight of her immediately made his throat dry: "Please, bring me a beer first," he croaked.
She laughed to herself as she walked away, bottom wiggling provocatively. She knew that the bow that held the short waitress' apron together emphasized her narrow waist and the movement of her small, round buttocks, which were visible under the tight, short skirt, and she felt that the guest's gaze was fixed on her.
Joe quickly picked something small from the menu so as not to delay the waiter too long and expressed his wish when she returned with his beer.
He had his consumption written to his room, gave Nilüfer, as her name c***d said, a three euro tip and wished her a good night.
Excited by the impressions in the restaurant, he took a quick shower and was just about to get his things ready for the next day when he heard a knock on his door.
With only a towel that he had wrapped around his waist in a hurry, he opened the

door a crack and looked into Nilüfer's black eyes. "Did I forget something?" he asked, puzzled. Beaming at him, she replied: "Yes, me…" and pushed the door open and pushed past him into his hotel room.

She walked purposefully towards the seating area at the back of the room, threw her large handbag onto an armchair and turned to him. She slowly pulled her white blouse out of her skirt, unbuttoned it and peeled it off provocatively. The towel tensed under the pressure of his erect penis, to which Nilüfer commented mischievously: "... it needs some space..." The white lace of her bra stood out sharply against the tan of her skin.

Dressed only in her white bra, black skirt and apron, she laughed and instructed Joe to sit on the bed and watch her.

Of course he obeyed the charming command - how could he otherwise?

Nilüfer unzipped her skirt and pulled it down until it slid to the floor of its own accord and she stepped out.

Protected from view by her white apron, she pulled down her panties and threw them in Joe's face. He caught the small, white thong and breathed in her intoxicating scent; she seemed to have freshly showered.

Finally she reached for the clasp of her bra, unclasped it and let it fall onto the chair. Pretty, small breasts with small brown areolas and erect nipples came to light... he felt the pulse pounding in his penis...
She came to the bed, only wearing her apron, and turned her wonderful little, round apple bottom towards Joe.
She whispered: "Now you can open the bow for me".
Joe stood up, pulled a ribbon, the bow fell to the floor, grabbed her small, firm breasts from behind with both hands and began to nibble her neck, her neck. His towel fell down so that she felt his piston against her back, at the level of her sweet butt dimples, and she turned around, reaching for him. "…but hello," she blurted out, sinking to her knees and bending him up against his stomach. She breathed very gently with the tip of her tongue along the shaft until she reached his glans. Nilüfer licked the head of his throbbing penis like a "popsicle" until she sucked the head into her wide open mouth and continued to swirl her tongue there, looking him directly in the eyes.
When Joe felt his juice rising, he withdrew from her hot oral cavity - he didn't want to

come yet - he wanted to give pleasure to this dark beauty first.

Nilüfer reached into her purse and pulled out a bottle of ipur lubricant and a condom package and lay down on the bed.

"Wow, you know your stuff," Joe remarked when he saw the anal lubricant and lay down next to her to immediately heat up her body with his mouth and tongue.

Nilüfer reached for the telephone with the words: "I still have to let you know that I'm finishing work now" and dialed the reception number. Beate picked up the call, quickly hung up the receiver, put up the "Reception no longer occupied" message and locked the hotel entrance door.

She quickly made her way to room 202 where she had accommodated her "dream man", the only room with a king-size bed and a full-length mattress.

She opened the door quietly with her passez-partout key and crept down the corridor into the room. She saw Nilüfer lying on his back, clawing at his hair and holding his face firmly against her privates, heard her moans and watched, coming closer, as he drove her friend to climax with quick flicks of his tongue around her clit.

She quietly placed her handbag next to the bed, took off her clothes completely and then climbed onto the mattress with the two of them. Joe started and let his eyes wander down Beate's body and back up again, then smiled at her and sucked one of her erect nipples between his lips.

Once again he devoted himself to Nilüfer's leaking love cave, he licked up the escaping love juice and again flicked her little, bulging pleasure pearl. Only now and then did he stick his tongue directly into the entrance to her boiling pleasure cave.

Beate swung herself over Nilüfer's face and watched Joe as he plowed her friend's labia with his tongue and drilled into her. She reached with her hand to Nilüfer's pussy, stroked through the wet, small labia and spread her fingers slightly so that Joe now had the opened, fleshy pink pussy between her brown labia in front of him.

Nilüfer immediately began licking her friend's already wet pussy lips , her pussy entrance and her little pink rosette in view. With her hands she pulled Beate's plump buttocks apart and, while letting her tongue warble between her labia, pushed the tip of her nose into the narrow back entrance, where she

knew that, like her, no man had ever penetrated.
She loved the taste of her friend's abundant love juice, her scent, sucked it in eagerly, felt how Beate's vaginal muscles began to twitch and drilled her bottom with a finger covered in her juices and saliva. Beate gasped out her first climax and she also felt her abdomen cramping up only to release itself again in the orgasm wave, she literally screamed her climax into Beate's pleasure cave...
Nilüfer's legs wanted to close, they squeezed Joe's head while he continued to lick her unabated until she went wild.
Then he reached for Beate, pulled her away from Nilüfer's face and laid the young woman next to her friend. He let a few drops of the lubricant run between her large breasts and swung himself over her, pressing his hard penis into the valley of these two balls of joy while Nilüfer squeezed her friend's breasts together.
Joe hadn't had a woman with such big breasts for a long time, he just had to have it "Spanish" again. Every time he came out of the valley with his swollen glans, Beate's tongue would flick out and lick the tip of his

penis, or Nilüfer would suck it into her hot mouth and circle it with her tongue.
He wouldn't be able to stand this for long, Joe realized and withdrew.
"Love each other as if I weren't there," demanded Joe and Nilüfer immediately climbed over Beate to do the 69 with her lying across the bed.
He first took a long look at the women as they pampered each other's bodies with a certainty that suggested that this was not the first time they had made love to each other.
Beate's slim but voluptuous white body turned under her friend's caresses. She had spread her legs wide, held by Nilüfer's arms and thus offered a view of her open, leaking vagina, whose labia were pulled apart by skilled fingers and onto her small, wrinkled butthole, over which her love juice, mixed with her friend's saliva, flowed.
Joe just had to grab hold of her, kneaded her womanly, round buttocks, got on his knees, licked the rosette up to the pubic area, Nilüfer's tongue and his tongue met, circled each other and separated again in the will to give Beate the highest pleasure.
While Nilüfer concentrated again on the clit and the increasingly twitching labia, Joe

turned his attention to the tight back door. He gently stroked the rosette with the tip of his tongue, which sent one shiver after another through Beate's body, until he now drilled his tongue into it, pulling her butt cheeks firmly apart.

He heard: "...yeah, ..., cool, oooh..." and finally fucked the small muscle ring with his tongue.

Then he stood up and walked to the other side.

He saw Beate's face, framed by Nilüfer's slim, brown legs, as she played around her friend's love pearl with her tongue. Her hands held her brown little buttocks spread and she ran her thumb through the gap every now and then, spreading the love juice.

Joe enjoyed the sight of Nilüfer's brown, girlish, little bottom and first licked her tight, firm buttocks, through her crack, and drilled his tongue into her cunt entrance, her tiny, brown rosette right in front of his eyes. "Just go to my handbag and get me the vibes…" Beate whispered.

He reached in and was amazed when he found a normal-shaped vib, a slim anal plug and a silicone-covered anal ball chain, with increasingly thicker balls at the end, as well as a tiny anal suppository with a vibration function attached to one short cable had its control.

Beate chose the vibrator when Joe showed her the range and ran it through Nilüfer's pleasure crack, switched it on and slowly pushed it into her vagina while continuing to lick her clit.

"Aaaah... Now it was Beate who was lying on top of Nilüfer, her white, plump, womanly bottom sticking up, sandwiched between her legs, the black-haired head of her friend who had sucked her pearl between her lips.

Joe took the anal suppository, switched it on and pressed it between Beate's fleshy labia, which were slippery with love juice, pulled it back on the cord and let it disappear back into her cave.

He gently bit her buttocks and massaged her back entrance, then pulled the suppository out of the vagina, made it slippery with the lubricating oil and drilled it through the sphincter. With his middle finger he penetrated her vagina, felt the vibration, massaged it from the inside and then bent his fingers upwards so that he moved the suppository through the thin skin that separates the front pleasure cave from the anus.

Thanks to her friend's loving treatment, Beate came closer to orgasm. Joe took the anal ball chain, smeared it generously with the lubricating oil, pulled out the suppository and pushed the first ball in. Her abdomen began to twitch and he pushed the next, slightly larger ball into the tight butt hole, which expanded under the pressure and closed again behind it after the ball was over the thickest point. Her friend had done this to her so many times, she knew the pain of stretching, the feeling of urgently needing to go to the bathroom - and she enjoyed it, knowing that she would soon experience a mega orgasm.

The fifth ball that Joe pushed into Beate's back door was already the diameter of a table tennis ball, she screamed and panted when it finally passed her sphincter. There must have been around twelve centimeters in her ass, but Joe followed up with the sixth and final ball, which was almost as big as a billiard ball, and slowly pushed it in while she raged under him.

The ring muscle was stretched to breaking point, showing white under the skin when he finally let the huge ball pass. She didn't go in far enough, so the butt hole remained open. Beate whimpered, screamed, screamed and, thanks to Nilüfer's tongue massage, reached the longed-for orgasm that made her rage and twitch. Joe pulled on the band and under tension, one ball after another popped out of her bottom, which remained open like a jagged crater.

He quickly grabbed a condom from the pack Nilüfer had brought with him. When he saw that they were HT condoms, which were particularly thick-walled and durable, and therefore intended for anal intercourse, he had to smile. Yes, it would take a little longer, he thought and rolled the rubber over his penis.

Joe ran the seat of his index finger over the jagged edge, massaging her slowly tightening anus from the inside before he moved in and placed his glans between her labia, which were covered in foam with love juice and lubricating oil.

He slowly slid in, feeling the contraction twitches of her vaginal muscles gripping his shaft, massaging and fucking slowly, using the entire length of his piston.

"No, don't go in there... that's my love hole," Nilüfer complained and Joe withdrew. "Yes, please, fuck me in there, please..." Joe heard Beate's voice and pushed in again: "Yesss, aaahrrrr, ..., yessss, yes, yes, arrrr, ...". Nilüfers watched from below as Joe's penis forced itself into her friend's pleasure crack, grabbed it and pulled it out to place it at the other entrance.

He pressed his glans into her anus, which had closed completely again. After his thick glans had passed the muscle ring, he slowly slid all the way into the hot tightness. He pressed his loins against his round, plump buttocks and stayed until Beate got used to the thickness and length of his cock and then started fucking in slow motion. Very slowly he withdrew his penis until his glans pulled the muscle ring outwards and slid it in again, just as slowly until it stopped, over and over again...

Not yet recovered from her orgasm, Beate felt her abdomen tense up again, another climax looming that now overwhelmed her. The trembling, twitching muscle of the butt entrance, which massaged Joe's shaft, caused his juices to rise, despite the sensation-reducing condom. Slowly, so as

not to cum, he pulled out his penis and replaced it with the penis-like vibrator that he pulled out of Nilüfer's vagina.
He stirred the full length of the vibrating pleasure rod into Beate's butthole, digging into her depths. She jerked her head back, panted and raved, twitched and shrieked: "Oooh, God,…., arrrrr…, aah, ooohh, …", rolled away from her dark friend and collapsed, exhausted, lying on her back. Nilüfer stood up and reached for Joe's hard, bobbing penis, pulled him towards him, unrolled the condom and carelessly threw it on the floor. "…beni sikmek…, …beni itmek, …beni sevismek…" she breathed and laughed at him: "Sana yalvar?yorum". She leaned down and licked his sticky glans, tasting her friend's love juice and translating what she said in Turkish as she looked into his questioning face: "Fuck me, push me, love me, I'm begging you" and sucked then put his penis in his mouth.
Joe lay down on the bed and asked the dark beauty to ride him. After rolling a new condom over his lance, she swung herself over him, guided his glans to her small labia and slowly lowered herself down. She opened her eyes and screamed as Joe's

penis stretched her, it hurt so big she felt his cock sliding inside her. He felt how tight she was, tighter than some of the buttholes he had pushed into, felt her heat, her wet grip, and lay there completely still.

He tenderly caressed her small brown breasts, gently rubbing the hard little nipples as she slid further down his trunk. With his shaft about halfway buried, she screamed again: "Asiri!!! ...too deep!!!" and wanted to stand up again, but Joe pulled her forward and held her against him by her buttocks. He gently circled his pelvis and fucked her lightly, always just until he hit her cervix. He was stroking her puckered back entrance with a finger to distract her a little from the supposed stretching pain, when he suddenly felt Beate's tongue playing with his finger and her friend's anus.

"…tatmin etmek,…, evet, …, beni yalamak,…" (…satisfy me, yes, lick me…) Nilüfer shouted as she was shaken hard by a climax and bit Joe on the chest, causing it to bleed slightly .

He pulled his penis out of the pulsating heat and pushed himself out from under the girl, maneuvering her so that he could take her from behind, lubricating her butt crack and

drilling his middle finger into her tight butt hole. "Evet, ..., evet, yes.
Much tighter than her friend's butt entrance, the sphincter tightened around Joe's finger. Nilüfer grimaced in pain, but was distracted by Beate's loving treatment.
She stroked her friend's dripping labia, played around her clit with a finger and gently bit her little buttocks.
With her other hand she ran over and under the girl's slim body, massaging her small breasts, her neck, everything she could reach.
Joe turned his hand, let his massaging fingers circle inside her, making her more and more supple and then placed his glans on the slightly open butt hole.
"You'll never get it in there," said Beate, who knew what Joe's penis had felt like in her back entrance and how its size had first caused her pain and later pleasure.
He was just about to withdraw again when Nilüfer shouted: "Evet,..., sikmek benim popo, ...yes, fuck my bottom,..." and he started his piston again.
The small butt hole slowly opened and he forced his glans into it, millimeter by millimeter. For Nilüfer it felt as if a tennis ball

had been pushed into her. She flinched back and wanted to avoid the huge intruder, but Beate held her tight and pulled her buttocks apart even tighter. His penis advanced further and further, with the girl's constant whining, until he was halfway inside her and waited there until the inner gate had also relaxed. The girl's bottom gripped his penis painfully tightly; he noticed that the hard grip would squeeze his blood out of his shaft if he didn't start slowly with fucking movements. Until his glans stretched out the girl's ring of muscle and she cried out, he pulled his cock out of her tight crater and slowly pushed it back in. Each time he got a little deeper until he was finally able to get all the way into this beautiful little butt. Nilüfer felt like she was being impaled; the depth of the piston in her stomach, in addition to the pain, made her sick. But she wanted to endure it, she had just seen her friend taking the entire length of the huge pole, she too wanted to reach the peak of pleasure. Still, she felt like she was breaking.

She felt that Beate had laid down under her again, enjoyed how her friend was licking her pleasure crack again, and concentrated on it to distract from the pain.

She felt the friction of his pole inside her, the feelings it caused were indescribable, as he slowly increased the pace and rammed harder and harder into her. She heard his sounds of pleasure, knew that it would finally come soon for him too - and came with such force that it went black before her eyes. Her twitching pushed Joe's penis out of her bottom, a painful emptiness arose within her, she panted, yelped, moaned, screamed, half in Turkish, half in German, while Beate sucked on her clitoris.

Nilüfer broke free, turned around, pushed Joe onto his back and, with his head between her legs, pounced on his penis. She tore off the condom and sucked the bulb far between her lips, into her hot, wet oral cavity, while Beate, who had joined, alternately sucked in his testicles and stuck a slippery finger into his bottom.

The sight of the dilated pink rosette in the brown, small bottom, which, like the entrance to the vagina, twitched incessantly, the hands that rubbed his shaft, the hot mouths that sucked his penis, the fingers that massaged his prostate, left him with it unexpected violence will come.

Joe felt his loins tighten, his stomach begin to bubble, and he felt his first spurt into a hot oral cavity. He didn't know which lips were surrounding him, were they Nilüfer's or Beate's, taking turns sucking in his twitching penis.

When he couldn't take it anymore, he pushed himself out of the hold, his flaccid penis glowing.

"How does it feel when you pump your seed into my ass? I want to feel that," said Nilüfer to the still dazed Joe.

"Give me a little time," he groaned, "my little one will give you a break, please pamper yourself a little more."

"We're going to take a shower first," laughed Beate, "Are you coming with us?"

"I'll come right away, it's okay," laughed Joe and looked after the two women, who couldn't be more different.

He must have drifted off when he woke up feeling the two women caressing his slowly erect penis with their tongues.

Laughing, they showed Joe their provocative buttocks, Beate had the vibrator in hers, and Nilüfers had the anal plug in hers. To heat it up further, they pulled their buttocks apart, wiggled their backsides seductively and fucked each other with the love toys, which they pulled out and pushed back in again.

"Me first," called Beate, who had gone into the doggy position so that he could now fuck her without a condom.

Joe straightened up, stood behind her, pressed his cock into the hot flesh and slid in all the way. Nilüfer took the same position right next to her friend, so that Joe pulled his penis out of Beate and forced it into her little brown bottom while the girls rubbed and stroked their own clits.

Again and again he fucked first one bottom, then the other, accompanied by the moans and screams of both women. Beate came first, her butthole clenched, his piston slipped out, she twitched and finished herself off by continuing to stimulate her clit.

Now he pushed into Nilüfer's tight butt crater, pulled her up so that she was kneeling upright in front of him, and fucked her deep towards her stomach. When Nilüfer climaxed in a scream, it was time for him too, he pumped his boiling lava, scorching his tube from the inside, deep into her intestines.

She felt his bubbling semen spurt into her in countless spurts, felt the heat, an unknown bliss flowing through her.

Joe slid himself into the spooning position with her and twitchingly pumped a few more loads into her bottom until his flaccid penis slid out with a smack.
She didn't care that his seed was bubbling out of her, running down her buttocks and thighs and spilling it, she was in seventh heaven in his strong arms.
She knew that next time she wouldn't want to share him with Beate, she would want him alone.
"Even if I can't sit for days afterwards," she laughed to herself.
Beate was also still lying on the bed, one hand on her pubic area, the other hand on her abused butthole and was still floating on cloud nine.
So the three of them fell asleep until Joe's alarm woke them all awake the next morning.
They smiled at each other. Joe got up and went to shower. When he came back, Beate and Nilüfers had already left. He got dressed and went to the restaurant for breakfast.
Then he had to go to work. Beate and Nilüfers stood at the reception and smiled. They said goodbye with the words "See you next time." All three grinned.

HOTELBOY

During the semester break I had already worked as a "boy" in a hotel several times. Depending on the shift, I was responsible for welcoming guests, luggage, errands and room service. Basically, I was a "do-anything girl," but I was happy with the job because there were hardly any tasks that were unpleasant.

I actually preferred the day shifts, but I couldn't avoid being assigned to the night shift from time to time. Same this time too. I was just coming back from the toilet when my colleague at the reception greeted me with the words: "A lady just arrived who wanted to order a midnight snack. You can then bring it to her room. No. 666." I just replied: "Ok, tell the kitchen to get in touch."

I was actually quite happy about the change; hanging around at reception was starting to get on my nerves. I was also hoping for a big tip, since guests who arrived late often skipped a lot if they were still being entertained.

About fifteen minutes later I made my way to the kitchen and then made my way to the room with a tray cart.

The "midnight snack" filled the entire car: a large bottle of champagne lay in an ice bucket, a large meal was kept warm in silver bowls, and it seemed as if there was also dessert.

I was about to knock on the door a second time when I heard a voice call out, "It's open! Come in!" I drove the car into the room, which still had hardly any traces of a guest: the suitcases were not yet opened and were standing next to the large bed, the menu for this week was open next to the telephone and on the large table There was a handbag and a cell phone in the window, from which you had a beautiful view of the Rhine.

I maneuvered the cart over to the table and waited a moment.

From the bathroom I heard that voice again, which sounded deep but warm: "Please put it on the table, I'll be right there." I did as I was told and when I was almost finished, I had the feeling that I was being watched from behind to become. I turned around and had to hold myself together not to let my thoughts show.

Standing in front of me was a stunning looking black woman. She still had wet, black, shoulder-length hair, was wearing a silk bathrobe and smiled at me with amusement.
The robe was not tied tightly so that the skin from the neck down could be clearly seen and the large breasts were half visible. Long, slender legs were visible under the bathrobe and the whole sight was simply stunning. The black woman had undoubtedly noticed my looks, but didn't show anything else, but went to the table and said playfully: "Well, then let's see what delicious things you brought me." She went to the table and lifted the lids one after the other up, looked at me and smiled: "Hmm, that's all very nice, but I'm not hungry at the moment!" She looked at me meaningfully and began to open the champagne bottle. She poured two glasses and handed one to me. I cleared my throat: "I'm not allowed to drink anything on duty and I should actually go back downstairs now."
She didn't care about it, but said challengingly: "You're there to ensure that your guests have a pleasant time here and are satisfied." The way she pronounced "satisfied" sent a shiver down my spine.

"Besides, you want a decent tip. So make me happy and toast with me and help me find my way here."

I hesitantly took the glass, she toasted me and smiled constantly.

Then she walked past me very slowly, and the swing of her hips showed so much practice that I inevitably turned to her. She sat on the edge of the bed and crossed her long, slender legs. "So, I only have time to see the city tomorrow, what could I do?" I was about to start telling her about the city's sights when she interrupted me: "Why are you standing, sit down come to me!" It wasn't a request, but an order. There was a cutting edge to her voice that suggested she was used to giving orders and there was no question that they would be followed.

I slowly walked over and sat next to her nervously. As soon as I sat down, she took my glass from me, placed it next to the bed and pushed me back so that I was lying on my back. She smiled at me as she ran her fingernails across my chest. "Well, before you give me long lectures about all the boring things I could do, maybe you'd better tell me where I can find hunky young men who will submit to me unconditionally."

As she said this, she ran her hand down my stomach and boldly reached between my legs as she said the last word. I bucked up and moaned because she immediately had my stiff cock in her hand through my pants. She just smiled and continued massaging my crotch. "Maybe it's better if you don't say anything at all." She unzipped my pants and while she massaged my steel-hard cock through my panties, she pushed up my shirt and began to tease my nipples with her long tongue.

As she continued as if it were the most normal thing in the world, my mind was spinning. I couldn't believe what was happening to me and even less could believe that I wasn't resisting it at all. When she bit my nipple, I groaned and looked into her face.

Her expression was a mixture of excitement and malice, as if she knew how I was feeling. On the one hand, everything in me wanted to end this game quickly, but on the other hand, I wanted nothing more than for her to continue.

She slid between my legs, took off my pants and panties, and I took off my shirt without hesitation at her request. She grabbed my stiff cock, pulled the foreskin all the way back with a quick jerk and squeezed my balls tightly.

I moaned loudly and was in heaven as she took my cock deep into her mouth and started sucking my cock hard. I moaned louder and louder, regardless of whether she was taking my cock all the way back into her mouth or whether she was squeezing my balls hard and pulling them down quickly. My whole body seemed to be one erection, completely dependent on her touch.

I didn't think she could arouse me any more, but when I felt her finger touch my rosette , I knew I was wrong. She naturally stuck her finger in my ass and clearly enjoyed the way I responded to this excitement. I groaned, "Oh, God, yesss, go on!"

Even though she didn't answer, she started sticking two fingers in my ass again and again. I moaned, squirmed and wanted nothing more than for her to never stop again.

As soon as I thought this thought in my excited trance, she stopped and sat on my chest. I opened my eyes and saw her smiling lustfully: "Well, sweetie, you seem to like my treatment. How about you return the favor now!"

With these words, which again were not a suggestion but an order, she opened her bathrobe.

At first I only saw her hot big tits, but what I saw made my blood run cold. A huge black stiff cock rose between her legs. I couldn't even think about what was going to happen because she pushed my head back and forced her cock into my mouth. I wanted to fight back, but my hands were trapped by her thighs. For a moment I was able to withstand the pressure on my mouth, but soon after I was unable to do anything other than let this monster cock into my mouth.

She moaned: "Yeah, you've been waiting for this all this time, you little slut!" She didn't realize in the slightest that I hadn't noticed the whole time that she was equipped with a cock instead of a pussy. She kept pressing my head between her legs so that her fat cock disappeared almost all the way into my mouth. We both moaned, although for different reasons. Her because she clearly enjoyed fucking my mouth with her huge cock - me because I still couldn't believe I was sucking a cock.

Despite my initial reluctance, I started to enjoy it and wanted practically nothing more than for her to push her fat black cock hard into my mouth again and again.
She actually did it for quite a while and while her cock was all the way in my mouth, she asked: "My sweetheart, I notice that you are starting to like it. If I get off you now to give you what you've always wanted to experience, will you submit to my orders or do I have to tie you up first ?" I just groaned in response and nodded.
As she got off me, I suspected what would inevitably follow, but I couldn't resist her commanding tone.
"Come on, get on all fours and show me your hot bubble butt!" I did as she was told, and as she knelt behind me and pulled my ass cheeks apart, I begged, "Please, be careful with your huge cock!"
But she didn't pay any attention to my pleas and instead pushed her huge, fat cock into my ass. For a moment I only saw stars, collapsed on the bed and screamed loudly. But she seemed to be in her element. She kept pushing her fat cock ALL THE WAY up my ass and moaning, "Yes, you little anal whore, you like that!" This is what you were

just waiting for!" I moaned, screamed, pleaded, begged, but again and again her monster cock ate into my ass and stretched it endlessly.

It was an incredibly intense mix of pain and pleasure. She started pushing her cock all the way up my ass again and again with hard thrusts so that her fat balls kept slapping against my butt. I moaned and screamed, but she didn't seem to want to stop.

When she started jerking my cock, I was done for. I moaned, "Yeah, fuck me!" Give it to me! Fuck me harder! Yes, deeper!"

She seemed happy to obey these requests and fucked me furiously while continuing to jerk my cock. With a loud scream I came in a real explosion. I was panting and completely exhausted when she suddenly stopped fucking me hard and threw me on my back. She sat on me, started jerking her cock and moaned: "Yessss, now you'll get your well-deserved tip, you little fuck slut!" I closed my eyes and just heard her moaning louder and louder. Suddenly she screamed and hot jets of her cum sprayed into my face. A jet hit me again and again, and with each one I groaned. Finally she stuck her cock into my sperm-covered mouth and gasped: "Lick it

clean, you horny piece!" I sucked her cock with relish and enjoyed the bitter, salty taste of her sperm in the back of my throat. Completely exhausted, she fell down next to me and said with a smile:
"If you agree to this form of payment, then I will have breakfast, lunch and dinner in the room tomorrow!"
I smiled back and said, "I have never been rewarded so richly! Besides, I'm actually on duty tomorrow!"
She lovingly stroked my cheek and breathed: "Great, that's sorted out then!" I'm going into the shower now. Stay there if you want, but I want to sleep alone !"
I lay on the bed dreaming for a few more minutes before getting dressed and quietly leaving the room. Anyone who had seen me from behind at that moment would have had no idea why I was dragging my feet, but I enjoyed every pain in my ass because it reminded me of my mistress's huge cock

about the author

Maria Valleetsy is a renowned author in the field of erotic literature, especially in the BDSM genre.

With her background as a sex therapist, she combines her in-depth knowledge of human sexuality with her passion for writing to create captivating and sensitive stories.

Her works are characterized by depth, carefully crafted characters, and an engaging portrayal of the BDSM world.

As an author, she seeks to explore not only the physical, but also the emotional and psychological dimensions of relationships and intimacy.

With her books, Maria Valleetsy inspires her readers to explore and understand their own sexual desires and boundaries.